Enjoy All of Beverly Cleary's Books
from Avon Camelot

And Don't Miss Beverly Cleary's Autobiography

BEVERLY CLEARY

MUGGIE MAGGIE

Illustrated by Alan Tiegreen

AN AVON CAMELOT BOOK

AVON BOOKS, INC.
1350 Avenue of the Americas
New York, New York 10019

Copyright © 1990 by Beverly Cleary
Interior illustrations by Alan Tiegreen
Published by arrangement with William Morrow and Company, Inc.
Library of Congress Catalog Card Number: 89-38959
ISBN: 0-380-71087-0
www.avonbooks.com

First Avon Camelot Printing: May 1991

CAMELOT TRADEMARK REG. U.S. PAT. OFF. AND IN OTHER COUNTRIES, MARCA REGISTRADA, HECHO EN U.S.A.

Printed in the U.S.A.

CW   32 33 34 35 36 37 38 39

_To a third-grade girl who wondered why
no one ever wrote a book to help
third graders read cursive writing_

Chapter 1

After her first day in the third grade, Maggie Schultz jumped off the school bus when it stopped at her corner. "Bye, Jo Ann," she called to the girl who was her best friend, sometimes. "See you tomorrow." Maggie was happy to escape from sixth-grade boys who called her a cootie and from fourth-grade boys who insisted the third grade was awful, cursive writing hard, and Mrs. Leeper, the teacher, mean.

Her dog, Kisser, was waiting for her. When Maggie knelt to hug him, Kisser licked her face. He was a young, eager dog the Schultzes had chosen from the S.P.C.A.'s Pick-a-Pet page in the newspaper. "A friendly cockapoo looking for a child to love" was the description under his picture, a description that proved to be right.

"Come on, Kisser." Maggie ran home with her fair hair flying and her dog springing along beside her.

When Maggie and Kisser burst through the kitchen door, her mother said, "Hi there, Angelface. How did things go today?" She held Kisser away from the refrigerator with her foot while she put away milk cartons and vegetables. Mrs. Schultz was good at standing on one foot because five mornings a week she taught exercise classes to overweight women.

"Mrs. Leeper is nice, sort of," began Maggie, "except she didn't make me a monitor and she put Jo Ann at a different table."

"Too bad," said Mrs. Schultz.

Maggie continued. "Courtney sits on one side of me and Kelly on the other and that Kirby Jones, who sits across from me, kept pushing the table into my stomach."

"And what did you do?" Mrs. Schultz was taking eggs out of a carton and setting them in the white plastic egg tray in the refrigerator.

"Pushed it back." Maggie thought a moment before she said, "Mrs. Leeper said we are going to have a happy third grade."

"That's nice." Mrs. Schultz smiled as she closed the refrigerator, but Maggie was doubtful about a teacher who forecast happiness.

How did she know? Still, Maggie wanted her teacher to be happy.

"Kisser needs exercise," Mrs. Schultz said. "Why don't you take him outside and give him a workout?" Maggie's mother thought everyone, dogs included, needed exercise.

Maggie enjoyed chasing Kisser around the backyard, ducking, dodging, and throwing a dirty tennis ball, wet with dog spit, for him until he collapsed, panting, and she was out of breath from running and laughing.

Refreshed and much more cheerful, Maggie was flipping through television channels with the remote control, trying to find funny commercials, when her father came home from work. "Daddy! Daddy!" she cried, running to meet him. He picked her up, kissed her, and asked, "How's my Goldilocks?" When he set her down, he kissed his wife.

"Tired?" Mrs. Schultz asked.

"Traffic gets worse every day," he answered.

"Was it your turn to make the coffee?" demanded Maggie.

"That's right," grumped Mr. Schultz, half-pretending.

Other than talking with people who came to see him, Maggie did not really understand what her father did in his office. She did know he made coffee every other day because Ms. Madden, his secretary, said she did not go to work in an office to make coffee. He should take his turn. Ms. Madden was such an excellent secretary—one who could spell, punctuate, and type—that Mr. Schultz put up with his share of coffee-making. Maggie found this so funny that she always asked about the coffee.

"Did Ms. Madden send me a present?" Maggie asked. Her father's secretary often sent

Maggie a little present: a tiny bottle of shampoo from a hotel, a free sample of perfume, and once, an eraser shaped like a duck. Maggie felt grown-up when she wrote thank-you notes on their home computer.

"Not today." Mr. Schultz tousled Maggie's hair and went to change into his jogging clothes.

When dinner was on the table and the family, exercised, happy, and hungry, was seated, Maggie chose the right moment to break her big news. "We start cursive this week," she said with a gusty sigh that was supposed to impress her parents with the hard work that lay ahead.

Instead, they laughed. Maggie was annoyed. Cursive was *serious*. She tossed her hair, which was perfect for tossing, waving and curling to her shoulders, the sort of hair that made women say, "What wouldn't you give for hair like that?" or, in sad voices, "I used to have hair that color."

"Don't look so gloomy," said Maggie's father. "You'll survive."

How did he know? Maggie scowled, still hurting from being laughed at, and said, "Cursive is dumb. It's all wrinkled and stuck together, and I can't see why I am supposed to do it." This was a new thought that popped into her mind that moment.

"Because everyone writes cursive," said Mrs. Schultz. "Or almost everybody."

"But I can write print, or I can use the computer," said Maggie, arguing mostly just to be arguing.

"I'm sure you'll enjoy cursive once you start," said Mrs. Schultz in that brisk, positive way that always made Maggie feel contrary.

I will not enjoy it, thought Maggie, and she

said, "All those loops and squiggles. I don't think I'll do it."

"Of course you will," said her father. "That's why you go to school."

This made Maggie even more contrary. "I'm not going to write cursive, and nobody can make me. So there."

"Ho-ho," said her mother so cheerfully that Maggie felt three times as contrary.

Mr. Schultz's smile flattened into a straight line. "Just get busy, do what your teacher says, and learn it."

The way her father spoke pushed Maggie further into contrariness. She stabbed her fork into her baked potato so the handle stood up straight, then she broke off a piece of her beef patty with her fingers and fed it to Kisser.

"Maggie, *please*," said her mother. "Your father has had a hard day, and I haven't had

such a great day myself." After teaching her exercise classes in the morning, Mrs. Schultz spent her afternoons running errands for her family: dry cleaner, bank, gas station, market, post office.

Maggie pulled her fork out of her baked potato. Kisser licked his chops and looked up at her with hope in his brown eyes, his tail wagging. "Kisser is lucky," she said. "He doesn't have to learn cursive." When her dog heard his name, he stood up and placed his front paws on her lap.

"Now you're being silly, Maggie," said her father. "Down, Kisser, you old nuisance."

Maggie was indignant. "Kisser is not a nūisance. Kisser is a loving dog," she informed her father.

"Don't try to change the subject." Mr. Schultz, irritated with Maggie, smiled at his wife, who was pouring him a cup of coffee.

"Books are not written in cursive," Maggie pointed out. "I can read chapter books, and not everyone in my class is good at that."

Mr. Schultz sipped his coffee. "True," he admitted, "but many things are written in cursive. Memos, many letters, grocery lists, checks, lots of things."

"I can write letters in printing, and I never write those other things," argued Maggie, "so *I am not going to learn cursive.*" She tossed her hair and asked to be excused.

Kisser felt that he, too, was excused. He trotted after Maggie and jumped up on her bed. As she hugged him, Maggie overheard her mother say, "I don't know what gets into Maggie. Most of the time she behaves herself, and then suddenly she doesn't."

"Contrary kid," said her father.

Chapter 2

The next day, after the third-grade monitors had led the flag salute, changed the date on the calendar, fed the hamster, and done all the housekeeping chores that third-grade monitors do in the morning, Mrs. Leeper faced her class and said, "Today is going to be a happy day."

The third grade looked hopeful.

"Today we take a big step in growing up,"

said Mrs. Leeper. "We are going to learn cursive handwriting. We are going to learn to make our letters flow together." Mrs. Leeper made *flow* sound like a long, long word as she waved her hand in a graceful flowing motion.

She calls that exciting, thought Maggie, slumping in her chair.

"How many of you have ridden on a roller coaster?" asked Mrs. Leeper. Half the members of the class raised their hands. Mrs. Leeper wrote on the chalkboard:

$$a \quad c \quad d \quad m \quad n$$

"Many letters start up slowly, just like a roller coaster, and then drop down," she said, and she traced over the first stroke of each letter with colored chalk. Then she went on to demonstrate how the roller coaster climbed almost straight up:

— — — · · · — — —

b f l t

After the paper monitor passed out paper, the class practiced, not whole letters but roller-coaster strokes:

ⵔ ⵔ ⵔ   ⵍⵍⵍ

Maggie did as she was told until she grew bored and began to draw one long roller-coaster line that rose and fell, turned and twisted, and rose again. So many of the class needed help with their strokes that Mrs. Leeper did not get around to Maggie.

The next day, after strokes, the class practiced whole letters, some with loops that went up, some with loops that went down. This was difficult. The third grade frowned, worried, struggled, and asked Mrs. Leeper whether they were doing it right. Then they learned to connect letters with straight lines. Maggie went on drawing roller coasters until Mrs. Leeper noticed.

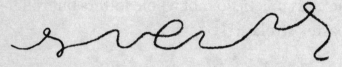

"Why, Maggie," she said, "why haven't you been working on your loops and lines?"

"I am working," said Maggie, "on roller coasters."

Mrs. Leeper looked thoughtfully at Maggie, who tried to look happy. "Roller coasters are not cursive," said the teacher.

"I know," agreed Maggie, "but I don't need cursive. I use our computer."

"Maggie, I think you had better stay after school so we can have a little talk," said Mrs. Leeper.

"I have to catch my bus," said Maggie with her sweetest smile.

That afternoon, Maggie examined cursive writing wherever she found it. "Why does your writing on the grocery list lean over backward?" she asked her mother. "Mrs. Leeper says letters should lean forward as if they were walking against the wind."

"I'm left-handed, and my teachers didn't show me how to turn my paper," answered Mrs. Schultz.

"And what are those little circles floating around?" asked Maggie.

Her mother laughed. "When I was in junior high, girls often made circles instead of dots over their *i*'s. We thought it was artistic or something. I don't really remember."

That evening, Maggie stood at her father's side as he wrote a letter on the computer. When he pulled the paper out of the printer,

he picked up a pen and wrote at the bottom:

Sydney Schultz

"What does that say?" asked Maggie.

"That's how I sign my name," said her father. "Sydney Schultz."

"You didn't close your loops," Maggie pointed out. "You are supposed to close loops on letters that have pieces that hang down." She had learned a thing or two in spite of herself.

"Oops," said Mr. Schultz, and he closed his loops.

Chapter 3

Maggie began to enjoy cursive time. She experimented with letters leaning over backward and decorated with little circles, the way her mother dotted her *i*'s. She wrote messy *g*'s with long straight tails, the way her father made his *y*'s.

"Why, Maggie," said Mrs. Leeper. "I find your cursive very untidy."

"I'm writing like a grown-up," Maggie explained.

The result was Mrs. Leeper's asking Maggie's mother to come to school for a conference. That day, Mrs. Schultz had to fill the gas tank of the car, go to the bank, buy paper for the computer, and take Kisser to the veterinarian for his shot—all this after teaching exercise classes in the morning. She was not smiling when she reached school, still wearing her warm-up suit. She handed Kisser's leash to Maggie so she could take care of him during her conference with Mrs. Leeper.

Kisser was so happy to see a playground full of children that he wanted to jump up on everyone. Maggie had to hold on to his leash with both hands when her friends gathered around to ask why Mrs. Schultz was talking to the teacher.

Jo Ann answered for Maggie. "Maybe Mrs.

Leeper wants her to be room mother or something."

"I bet," said Kirby on his way to the bus.

"What did she say?" demanded Maggie when her mother returned and everyone had boarded buses. "What did Mrs. Leeper say about me?"

"Down, Kisser!" Mrs. Schultz sounded cross. "Mrs. Leeper said you are a reluctant cursive writer who has not reached cursive-writing readiness, and perhaps you are too immature to write it."

Maggie was indignant. "I am not!" she said. "I am Gifted and Talented." Some people were Gifted and Talented, and some people weren't. At least, that was what teachers thought. Maybe no one had told Mrs. Leeper how Gifted and Talented she was. Maggie's mother drove home without saying one single word. Maggie hugged Kisser, who was so grateful that he licked her face, which she found comforting. Someone loved her.

For several days, just for fun, Maggie drew fancy letters at cursive time, and then Mrs. Leeper told her that Mr. Galloway, the principal, wanted to see her in his office. On her way, Maggie, filled with dread, dawdled as long as she felt she could get away with it.

"Hello there, Maggie," said Mr. Galloway. "Sit down and let's have a little talk."

Maggie sat. She never enjoyed what grown-ups called "a little talk."

Mr. Galloway smiled, leaned back in his chair, and placed his fingertips together like an A, with his thumbs for the crossbar. A printed A, of course. "Maggie, Mrs. Leeper tells me you are not writing cursive. Can you tell me why?"

Maggie swung her legs, stared at a picture of George Washington on the wall, nibbled a

hangnail. Mr. Galloway waited. Finally, Maggie had to say something. "I don't want to."

"I see." Mr. Galloway spoke as if Maggie had said something very important that required serious thought, lots of it.

"And why don't you want to?" asked the principal after a long silence, during which Maggie studied the way he combed his hair over his bald spot.

"I just don't want to," said Maggie. "I use a computer."

Mr. Galloway nodded as if he understood. "That's all, Maggie," he said. "Thank you for coming in."

That evening, Mrs. Leeper telephoned Maggie's mother to say that the principal had reported Maggie was not motivated to write cursive. "That means you don't want to," Mrs. Schultz explained to Maggie.

"That's what I told him," said Maggie, who couldn't see what all the fuss was about.

"Maggie!" cried her mother. "What are we going to do with you?"

"I'll motivate you, young lady," said Mr. Schultz. "No more computer for you. You stay strictly away from it."

Mrs. Schultz had more to say. "Tomorrow, Maggie is to see the school psychologist." She looked worried, Mr. Schultz looked grim, and Maggie was frightened. A psychologist sounded scary. Kisser understood. He licked Maggie's hand to make her feel better.

As it turned out, Maggie loved the psychologist, who talked in a quiet voice and let her play with some toys while he asked gentle questions about her family, her dog, her teachers—nothing important. He asked about her times tables, and almost as an afterthought, he inquired, "How do you like cursive writing?"

"Okay," answered Maggie, because he was a grown-up.

A couple of days later, Maggie's mother said, "The school psychologist wrote us a letter."

Maggie's feelings were hurt. He had seemed like such a nice man. She had learned to be suspicious of letters from school. This was not the first.

Mrs. Schultz continued. "He says it will be interesting to see how long it will take you to decide to write cursive."

"Oh," said Maggie.

"How long do you think that will be?" asked Mrs. Schultz.

"Maybe forever," said Maggie, beginning to wish she had never started the whole thing.

Chapter 4

Maggie had grown bored with not writing cursive, but by now the whole third grade was interested in her revolt. Each day, they watched to see whether she gave in. Her friends talked about it at lunchtime. In the hall, she overheard a fourth grader say, "There goes that girl who won't write cursive." Many people thought she was brave; others thought she was acting stupid. Obviously, Maggie could not back down now. She had to protect her pride.

Courtney and Kelly, best friends who sat opposite one another, did not approve of Maggie.

Courtney said, "Only first and second graders print."

Kelly said, "I think you are acting dumb, Maggie."

Jo Ann whispered from the next table. "If you are having trouble, maybe I can help you on Saturday."

"I'm *not* having trouble," Maggie whispered back. "I just don't want to do it." Then she worried. What if others thought Gifted and Talented Maggie couldn't write cursive if she wanted to?

Mrs. Leeper handed out individual papers with each person's name, first and last, written in perfect cursive at the top. "Today we practice our signatures," she said, and she looked at Maggie. "Even if we write letters on computers, we must sign them in our own handwriting."

Maggie studied her neatly written name. If she wrote "Maggie Schultz" and not one letter more, would this be giving in? Not really, she decided, not if she wrote like a grown-up.

While Kirby—a boy who always did what he was told, more or less—gripped his pencil, pressing down so hard he broke the point and had to go to the pencil sharpener, and Courtney and Kelly wrote with pencils whispering daintily across their papers, Maggie wrote her name the way her father wrote his:

Maggie Schultz

On the next line, she wrote with her left hand, which was difficult:

Maggie Schultz

Kirby worked so hard that he needed a rest. He pushed the table into Maggie's stomach. Maggie pushed it back.

"Mrs. Leeper!" said Courtney. "Kirby and Maggie are wrecking our cursive."

"They do it all the time," said Kelly.

This brought Mrs. Leeper to their table. "See, Mrs. Leeper," said Courtney, pointing. "That is where Kirby pushed the table."

"And this is where Maggie pushed it back," said Kelly.

"I'm sure they won't do it again." Mrs. Leeper tried to look happy as she paused beside Maggie.

Maggie quickly curved her arm around her paper and bowed her head as if she was working very, very hard.

Mrs. Leeper, who often told the class she had eyes in the back of her head, had already seen Maggie's work, if one could really call it work. "Maggie, why are you writing with your left hand when you are right-handed?" she wanted to know.

"That's the way my mother writes," explained Maggie.

Mrs. Leeper removed the pencil from Maggie's left hand and placed it in her right. "And where are the loops on your g's that we talked about? Your l and t are leaning over backward. We don't want our telephone poles to tip over, do we?"

"I guess not," said Maggie.

"Take your paper home and do it over," said

Mrs. Leeper, "and we must close our *a*. Your name is not Muggie."

Maggie knew she was done for.

"Muggie Maggie," whispered Kirby, as Maggie had expected.

"You keep quiet." Maggie pushed the table into his stomach.

"Mrs. Leeper!" cried Courtney and Kelly at the same time.

"I thought we were going to have a happy teacher today," said Mrs. Leeper. "Let's be good citizens."

Maggie was sure she would not have a happy recess, and she did not. Everyone shouted "Muggie Maggie! Muggie Maggie!" Kirby started it, of course. He was not a good citizen.

Chapter 5

Later that week, Mr. Schultz brought Maggie a present from Ms. Madden, a ball-point pen that wrote in either red or blue ink.

"Just what I've always wanted." Maggie was filled with love for Ms. Madden, the one grown-up who, Maggie felt, did not pick on her.

"Can I thank her on the computer?" asked Maggie, testing her father.

"You may not. The computer is off limits." Mr. Schultz was annoyingly cheerful. "Use your new pen."

Maggie was not surprised. Her father always meant what he said. She went to her room and, with Kisser resting his nose on her foot, went to work. Her printing was not as neat as it once had been because she was out of practice. She wrote one letter in blue, the next in red, over and over.

Dear Ms. Madden,
   Thank you for the pen. I like it.
            Love,
               Maggie

After a moment's thought, she added:

Sorry
Sloggy

There. Maggie, pleased with her work, folded the letter, sealed it in an envelope, printed Ms. Madden on the front, and slipped it into her father's briefcase, with the virtuous feeling of having done what was expected of her.

The next evening, Mr. Schultz brought home an envelope for Maggie, who tore it open. The note, as she had expected, was from Ms. Madden and was neatly typed, except for one consonant. It read:

Dear Maggie,
If you are really

$\int$ orry
o
loggy

(or did you mean sloppy?)
why didn't you copy your
letter over?
Love,

Hilda Madden

Maggie's eyes filled with tears, she felt so ashamed. Now even Ms. Madden, along with everyone else, was picking on her.

Mrs. Schultz, seeing Maggie's tears, asked to read the note. Then she said gently, "Well, Angelface, why didn't you do your letter over?"

Maggie sniffed. "I thought Ms. Madden would understand."

Maggie's father took his turn at reading the embarrassing note. "Of course Ms. Madden wouldn't understand," he said. "Ms. Madden is a secretary who is always neat and accurate."

"Well, I don't want to be a secretary," said Maggie, thinking of several neat, accurate girls in the third grade. "I'm going to be an astronaut or a meter maid."

"Good for you, Goldilocks," said her father, and he rumpled her hair.

Chapter 6

One morning, Maggie noticed Mrs. Leeper whispering with other teachers in the hall. They glanced at Maggie, who scrunched down, trying to look invisible so they wouldn't talk about her.

When class started, Mrs. Leeper said, "Boys and girls, let's have a happy teacher today." She said that so often, no one paid any atten-

tion. Then she pointed to words she had written on the chalkboard:

mouth of September
mice day

The words made the class laugh, but Maggie did not see anything funny. Mrs. Leeper said, "Maggie, can you tell us what is wrong with these words?"

That was the moment when Maggie discovered she could not read cursive. She shook her head while others, eager to point out errors, waved their hands.

Later in the day, Mrs. Leeper announced, "Class, we need a message monitor. Who wants to be our message monitor?"

Even though she did not expect to be chosen because she was not a person who made Mrs. Leeper happy, Maggie raised her hand. So did the rest of the class, except Kirby, who never wanted to be a monitor for anything and who, at the moment, was under the table.

"Maggie, you may be our message monitor," said Mrs. Leeper.

"She means Muggie," whispered Kirby, coming up from under the table, where he had been figuring out how the legs were fastened to the top.

"Me?" said Maggie.

"Yes, you," said Mrs. Leeper with a happy smile. "And here is a note for you to take to Mr. Galloway." She handed Maggie an envelope. "Please wait for an answer."

Maggie lost no time in escaping to the freedom of the hall, where no one supervised her. The envelope was not sealed. Peeking was cheating, Maggie told herself. Bravely and honestly, Maggie carried the note halfway to the principal's office. Then she stopped and thought, One peek won't hurt, not if it's quick. If the envelope was not sealed, it must be all right to look inside.

She might have guessed—cursive writing. Maggie could not figure out the note, which read:

When is this girl ever going to decide to write cursive?

Maggie recognized the question mark and decided Mrs. Leeper was probably asking for more work sheets or something equally boring.

"Hello there, Maggie," said the principal when she held out the note. While Maggie waited, Mr. Galloway wrote a short answer, which he put in the same envelope. He crossed out his name and wrote Mrs. Leeper's name in its place. The school could not afford to waste envelopes.

"Take this to your teacher," he said with a big smile. "And thank you, Maggie."

I won't look, I won't look, Maggie told herself. What would be the use when the note was written in cursive? Maggie walked more and more slowly. Was it wrong to look at something she could not read? Of course not, Maggie decided, and she slipped the note out of the envelope.

Mr. Galloway's cursive was not as neat as Mrs. Leeper's, which did not seem right to Maggie. A principal's writing should be better than a teacher's.

Maggie will decide to read and write cursive sooner or later. It looks like later.

Maggie studied Mr. Galloway's loops and curves until one word jumped out at her:

Maggie. She was shocked. What was Mr. Galloway saying about her? Maggie felt her cheeks turn red. Quickly, she replaced the note and hurried to her classroom as if she was carrying something hot. Mrs. Leeper gave her a sharp look and said, "Thank you, Maggie," before she read what the principal had written. Then she smiled, once more a happy teacher.

Suddenly, Maggie found cursive interesting. How could she read people's letters if she could not read cursive? She couldn't. Maggie, Gifted and Talented Maggie, felt defeat.

Chapter 7

For the next few days Maggie was a busy message monitor because Mrs. Leeper sent her hurrying to one room after another. She was even sent to the library. The envelope grew shabby. Most messages contained her name; others did not. Maggie snatched moments in the hall to try to figure out words, but all she learned was that some teachers were careless about joining letters without lifting pencil from paper.

"How come you're delivering so many messages?" asked Kirby.

"Because she can't read cursive," said Courtney.

"And Mrs. Leeper knows she can't snoop," said Kelly.

"Mrs. Leeper wants me to deliver them," said Maggie. "It makes her happy."

"I bet," said Kirby.

On her way to the first-grade room, Maggie discovered that all of Mrs. Leeper's notes looked exactly alike, which was funny peculiar, not funny ha-ha. Feeling big and important in front of first graders, Maggie wondered about this as she listened to the little children play with the Velcro fasteners on their shoes. *Rip-rip-rip*. This teacher's answer to Mrs. Leeper

did not contain her name, so Maggie was not much interested. It read:

Keep it up. You will wear this kid down yet.

In the sixth-grade room, Maggie felt as if she had shrunk because all the sixth graders stared at her while the teacher, a tall man with a ferocious beard, read the note.

"There's the cootie," she heard a boy whisper.

Maggie tossed her hair. The class tittered. Maggie wondered whether the boys called their teacher's beard a cootie motel.

The man glanced at Maggie, grinned, and wrote a note on the back of an old spelling test. Then he crossed out his name on the ragged envelope, replaced it with Mrs. Leeper's name in one of the few spaces left, and handed it to

Maggie, who was grateful to escape to the hall.

When she peeked, Maggie found her own name, just as she had in other notes, but this time she found it twice. The note read:

I once had a bright kid like Maggie who thought she couldn't read cursive She really could when she tried, but she wouldn't. Sounds like Maggie.

Maggie, desperate to read, discovered this teacher was careless about joining letters. If she had time, maybe she could puzzle them out, but she knew that she was expected back in her own classroom. Sending someone to find her would not make Mrs. Leeper happy.

Friday evening, Jo Ann telephoned to ask Maggie to spend the night at her house.

Maggie said she couldn't. Jo Ann wanted to know why. Maggie said she had to help her father.

"I thought he did some kind of office work," said Jo Ann.

"He does," said Maggie, thinking fast. "I know how to use our computer." She had not lied, not exactly, but she felt guilty.

That weekend, Maggie studied every bit of cursive writing she could find: her mother's tipping-over-backward grocery list, Ms. Madden's neat handwritten notes mixed in with papers her father brought home from the office, anything. She did not try to read her father's writing. She knew it was hopeless.

Maggie spent most of her time in her room with her door closed. With Kisser's nose resting on her foot and some old work papers in front of her, she frantically practiced cursive, including the difficult capitals: $\mathcal{Q}$ $\mathcal{W}$ $\mathcal{F}$

"What are you doing, Maggie?" asked her mother through the door.

"Nothing," answered Maggie, aware that her mother felt children were entitled to privacy and would not open the door. Letting her parents know she had changed her mind would make Maggie feel ashamed, like admitting she had been wrong.

Maggie worked hard, and by Sunday evening she agreed with what Mrs. Leeper had been saying all along: Many cursive letters are shaped like printed letters. She knew she could read cursive as long as it was neat. She practiced her signature with her letters leaning into the wind:

Maggie Schultz Maggie Schultz

When she had finished, Maggie's face was flushed, her hair more tousled than usual, but she could write cursive. Maybe it wasn't perfect, but anyone past the second grade could read it. She went to her father, who was working at the computer. "Daddy, listen to me," she said, and her voice was stern.

Mr. Schultz turned from the keyboard. "Okay, Maggie, what's up?"

"In writing, neatness counts," Maggie informed him.

"I expect it does," he agreed.

"Then you should learn to close your loops and put the right number of peaks on your *u*'s and write neatly," said Maggie.

"Funny, Ms. Madden says the same thing," said Mr. Schultz. "I'll try. Cross my heart."

Maggie was not sure she believed him. Next, Maggie went to her mother and announced, "You should make your writing lean the other way like it's supposed to and stop putting silly circles over your *i*'s."

Mrs. Schultz smiled and pushed Maggie's hair back from her flushed face. "I don't know about that, Angelface," she said. "Everyone says my handwriting is distinguished."

Maggie was tired and cross. "Well, it's wrong," she said, and she sighed so hard that Kisser looked anxious. Grown-ups were so hard to reform—maybe impossible.

Chapter 8

On Monday, Maggie looked at the words Mrs. Leeper had written on the chalkboard and discovered she was reading them because *she couldn't help it*. Mrs. Leeper had written:

This is going to be a happy week. We are going on a field trip.

Maggie was eager to carry the next message. She did not have to wait long for Mrs. Leeper to write a note for the principal. As soon as she closed the door—quietly, no slamming—Maggie slipped out the note that was written on the back of an old arithmetic paper and read the neatly formed words:

Maggie is now reading cursive. I saw her reading what I had written on the chalkboard. If she can read it, she can write it. She just won't admit it.

Maggie was shocked. Maggie was angry.

Mrs. Leeper had guessed she would peek. Maybe she had guessed all along, and now that Maggie could read cursive, she was saying mean things about her. But worst of all, Mrs. Leeper was waiting for an answer.

Maggie wanted to crumple the note, but if she did that, Mrs. Leeper would want to know why Mr. Galloway had not sent a reply. She returned the note to its tattered envelope, dragged her feet into the principal's office, and thrust it at him. She stood staring at the floor while he read it.

"Um-hm," he murmured, and Maggie heard his pen move across paper. "There you go, Maggie," he said as he handed the remains of the envelope back to her. "Thank you."

"You're welcome," said Maggie, and she got out of his office as fast as she could without running.

I won't peek, I won't peek, she told herself,

but of course, she finally had to peek. What normal third grader wouldn't want to know what the principal had to say in time of crisis? This note said:

Hooray! I can tell by the way she behaves that you are right. Good teaching, Laura! I knew you could do it.

Congratulations, Maggie!

Figuring out the long word before her name took a while, and then—well! First of all, Maggie was astonished that Mr. Galloway would call a teacher by her first name. Then Maggie was indignant. Mrs. Leeper hadn't done a thing. Maggie had done all the work, and now her teacher was getting all the credit.

Maggie dreaded returning to her classroom. She plodded along, trying to figure out how she could avoid it. She couldn't, not even if she took time to go to the bathroom. Sooner or later she had to face her teacher.

With red cheeks, she handed her teacher the remains of the envelope and was about to hurry to her seat when Mrs. Leeper caught her hand, pulled Maggie to her, gave her a big hug, and said, "I don't think we need a message monitor anymore. Anyway, the envelope is worn out." She tossed it, along with the note, into the wastebasket and said, "This is a happy day, Maggie."

Maggie was both pleased and confused. She had expected Mrs. Leeper to say something about cursive, but the teacher had not. She had not even said, "It's about time," or "I knew you could do it." She just smiled at Maggie, who finally felt she could smile back.

"You know something, Mrs. Leeper?" Maggie said shyly. "Your cursive is neater than any other teacher's cursive."

Mrs. Leeper laughed. "It has to be. I'm the one who teaches it."

Maggie walked slowly to her seat. She could now make her letters flow together, and she had made her teacher happy, but maybe when she grew up and did not have to please grown-ups all the time, she might decide not to write cursive. She could print anytime she wanted. She had plenty of time to think it over.

"Muggie Maggie," said Kirby. "Teacher's pet."

Maggie decided against pushing the table into his stomach.

Instead, she sat down and wrote a note in cursive, which she shoved across the table:

You stop pushing the table
into my stomick.

Sinseerly,
Maggie

Enter the World of Beverly Cleary

Beverly Cleary was born in McMinnville, Oregon, and until she was old enough to attend school she lived on a farm in Yamhill, a town so small it had no library. Her mother arranged to have books sent to their tiny town from the state library and acted as a librarian in a room over a bank. It was there that Mrs. Cleary learned to love books.

Generations of children have grown up with Ramona Quimby, Henry Huggins, Ralph S. Mouse, and all of their friends, families, and assorted pets. Beverly Cleary continues to capture the hearts and imaginations of children of all ages throughout the world.

Dear Mr. Henshaw

In this Newbery Award-winning book, a correspondence with his favorite author helps sixth-grader Leigh Botts deal with some tough problems—a new school, missing his dog Bandit, a lunch thief, and especially his parents' divorce.

Strider

In the sequel to the Newbery winner *Dear Mr. Henshaw,* Leigh Botts is down in the dumps. His parents have divorced and his dog has run away, and it doesn't look as if things could get any worse. But Leigh's life takes a turn for the better when he adopts a stray dog named Strider.

Beezus and Ramona

Beezus tries very hard to be patient with her little sister, but four-year-old Ramona has a habit of doing the most unpredictable, annoying, embarrassing things in the world. Sometimes Beezus doesn't like Ramona much, and that makes her feel very guilty. Sisters are supposed to love each other, but pesky little Ramona doesn't seem very lovable to Beezus right now.

Ramona the Pest

Ramona is off to kindergarten, and it is the greatest day of her life. She loves her teacher, Miss Binney, and she likes a little boy named Davy so much she wants to kiss him. So why does Ramona get in so much trouble? And how does Ramona manage to disrupt the whole class during rest time? Anyone who knows Ramona knows that she never *tries* to be a pest.

Ramona the Brave

Now that she's six and entering the first grade, Ramona is determined to be brave, but it's not always easy, with a scary new all-by-herself bedroom, her mother's new job, and a new teacher who just doesn't understand how hard Ramona is trying to grow up.

Ramona and Her Father

In this Newbery Honor Book, the whole family is grumpy when Mr. Quimby loses his job. Ramona keeps trying to cheer up her family, but every new idea seems to cause more trouble. Her sister and parents, even her teacher, seem to have lost their patience with Ramona. But when her father tells her he wouldn't trade her for a million dollars, Ramona knows everything will be okay.

Ramona and Her Mother

When Ramona's mother takes on a full-time job, there's trouble in the Quimby household. Seven-and-a-half-year-old Ramona feels unloved and starts twitching her nose like a rabbit, until her teacher becomes concerned.

Ramona Quimby, Age 8

Ramona feels quite grown up taking the bus by herself, helping big sister Beezus make dinner, and trying hard to be nice to pesky Willa Jean after school. Turning eight years old and entering the third grade can do that to a girl. So how can her teacher call her a nuisance? Being a member of the Quimby family in the third grade is harder than Ramona expected.

Ramona Forever

From the moment Howie Kemp's mysterious "rich" Uncle Hobart arrives from Saudi Arabia, life becomes more and more confusing. What's so special about Uncle Hobart, who only teases Ramona? And why are Ramona's mother and Aunt Bea keeping secrets? Life for Ramona is full of beginnings, discoveries, and surprises. But through all of the happiness and change, and some small moments of sadness, she's always wonderful Ramona—forever!

Henry Huggins

Henry Huggins had been wishing for some excitement in his life—but not this kind. There's no way he wants to stand on the school stage in his pajamas—and be kissed by an eighth-grade girl! Henry soon finds out that this is only the beginning of his exciting new life.

Henry and Ribsy

Henry Huggins is trying his hardest to keep Ribsy out of trouble for a whole month. But Ribsy doesn't make it easy for Henry. What can one boy do with a dog who steals a policeman's lunch and an ice cream cone from Ramona Quimby?

Henry and Beezus

All Henry Huggins can think about is owning a bicycle, especially since that big show-off Scooter McCarthy has one. Selling bubble gum to all the kids at school brings Henry plenty of trouble but very little money for his bike fund. Can a girl really help Henry earn the money for a bicycle? Henry's friend Beezus helps him turn the most humiliating situation of his life into a real business success.

Henry and the Clubhouse

Henry Huggins has a lot of good ideas when he first begins his paper route, especially the idea to build a clubhouse. Henry and his friends don't want any girls hanging out at their new clubhouse. But a silly old sign that says NO GIRLS ALLOWED can't stop Beezus and Ramona Quimby.

Henry and the Paper Route

Henry Huggins couldn't wait to turn eleven years old so he could have a paper route like his friend Scooter. He was sure he could prove that he was responsible enough to handle the job. But Henry is sidetracked by four lively kittens, one boy with a robot, and Ramona Quimby, the ever-present pest of Klickitat Street.

Ribsy

Poor Ribsy! Somehow he's gotten himself hopelessly lost in a huge shopping mall parking lot. Even worse, he ends up in the wrong family's car. Ribsy doesn't want to live in a house where three girls give him a bubble bath. All he wants to do is go home and be Henry Huggins's dog again. Instead, he's about to begin the liveliest adventure of his life!

The Mouse and the Motorcycle

Ralph only wanted to ride the mouse-sized motorcycle someone had left on the table in the hotel room where Ralph lived. Instead, both Ralph and the motorcycle take a terrible fall into the wastepaper basket, where they are trapped until Keith, the owner of the motorcycle, rescues them. Keith teaches Ralph to ride the motorcycle, and the two of them soon find out that adventures can be both fun and dangerous!

Runaway Ralph

Ralph has made up his mind—he is going to run away. Envisioning fun, freedom, and delicious crumbs from peanut-butter-and-jelly sandwiches, he hops on his red bike and zooms away to the summer camp down the road. Once he arrives, he runs headlong into a strict watchdog, a mouse-hungry cat, and even more fur-raising escapades. Suddenly home doesn't seem like a bad place to be.

Ralph S. Mouse

When Ralph's home at the Mountain View Inn is overrun by rowdy mice who want to use his red motorcycle, he packs up his prized machine and moves to a new home—inside Irwin J. Sneed Elementary School!

Ellen Tebbits

Ellen Tebbits believes she would die of embarrassment if any of the girls at school were to learn her secret. Then she meets Austine Allen, a new girl in class who is hiding the very same secret. They become best friends immediately, until Ellen slaps Austine in the middle of a crowded school lunchroom!

Otis Spofford

There is nothing Otis Spofford likes better than stirring up a little excitement. Otis also loves to tease Ellen Tebbits—probably because Ellen is so neat and clean, and she never fails to become angry. One day Otis's teasing goes a little too far, and now he is worried—because Ellen isn't just angry . . . she's planning something.

Emily's Runaway Imagination

Adventure is pretty scarce in Pitchfork, Oregon, so Emily keeps herself amused bleaching Dad's old plow horse and feeding the hogs an occasional treat. Then she decides that Pitchfork needs a library—and making it happen is the perfect challenge for a girl with a runaway imagination.

Muggie Maggie

When Maggie Schultz arbitrarily decides cursive writing is not for her, her rebellion gets her into trouble. Then Maggie becomes the message monitor, but she can't figure out what the teacher's notes say. Suddenly, Maggie finds cursive interesting. How can she read people's letters if she can't read cursive?

Socks

It was Socks's lucky day when he went to live with the Brickers. He got all of the attention he wanted. But that was before the Brickers came home with a new baby. Suddenly a crying little bundle is getting all of the attention, and Socks feels as if he's been replaced. What Socks doesn't know is that the baby is getting bigger every day and soon he will be joining Socks in all kinds of fun and mischief!

Mitch and Amy

Mitch and Amy are always squabbling about something. They think being twins is fun, but that's about the only thing they have in common—until the school bully starts picking on Mitch and Amy, too. Now the twins agree about one thing, and they can't waste any more time fighting with each other.

Fifteen

It seems too good to be true. The most popular boy in school has asked Jane out—and she's never even dated before. Stan is tall and good-looking, friendly and hard-working—everything Jane ever dreamed of. But is she ready for this? With warmth, perceptiveness, and humor, Beverly Cleary chronicles the joys and worries of a girl's first crush.

Jean and Johnny

It should be the happiest moment of Jean's life—instead of the most embarrassing. Why couldn't she have been ready when the best-looking, most popular boy in school asked her to dance? Instead she is stepping all over his feet and is completely tongue-tied. Despite her family's warning about chasing the handsome Johnny Chessler, Jean has to learn from experience the perils of a one-sided romance.

The Luckiest Girl

Shelley's spending the winter in California, and she feels as if she's living in a fantasyland. Now the star of the school basketball team is smiling at her, and all of the other girls are green with envy. Shelley feels like the luckiest girl in the world. She's about to discover the magic of falling in love—and a whole lot more!

Sister of the Bride

Barbara can hardly believe her older sister is getting married. With all of the excitement, Barbara can't help

dreaming of the day she will be the bride. But as the big day draws near and her sister turns suddenly apprehensive, the sister of the bride finds herself having second thoughts about running into love.

A Girl from Yamhill

In the first volume of her autobiography, Beverly Cleary shares the fascinating story of her life. She recalls her early years as a child growing up on a rural farm and later on her beloved Klickitat Street in Portland, Oregon, the setting for many of her stories.

My Own Two Feet

The girl from Yamhill grows up. In the second volume of her autobiography, Beverly Cleary shares with her readers the origins of her early career. Cleary brings to life her memories of leaving home, her beginnings as a writer, and the wonderful moment when she sold her first book, *Henry Huggins*.

There are more Ramona
adventures to share!

RAMONA'S WORLD
Beverly Cleary

Have you read it?
It's new. Don't miss it.

Ramona's World, the long-
awaited new book about the
irresistible, irrepressible
Ramona Quimby, star of
Beverly Cleary's best-loved
and best-selling series.
Ramona's in the fourth grade
now, with brown hair, brown
eyes, no cavities, a new baby
sister and a new best friend!

BEW 0799

Read All the Stories by
Beverly Cleary

☐ **HENRY HUGGINS**
70912-0 ($4.99 US/ $6.99 Can)

☐ **HENRY AND BEEZUS**
70914-7 ($4.99 US/ $6.99 Can)

☐ **HENRY AND THE CLUBHOUSE**
70915-5 ($4.99 US/ $6.99 Can)

☐ **ELLEN TEBBITS**
70913-9 ($4.99 US/ $6.99 Can)

☑ **HENRY AND RIBSY**
70917-1 ($4.99 US/ $6.99 Can)

☐ **BEEZUS AND RAMONA**
70918-X ($4.99 US/ $6.99 Can)

☑ **RAMONA AND HER FATHER**
70916-3 ($4.99 US/ $6.99 Can)

☐ **MITCH AND AMY**
70925-2 ($4.99 US/ $6.50 Can)

☐ **RUNAWAY RALPH**
70953-8 ($4.99 US/ $6.99 Can)

☑ **RAMONA QUIMBY, AGE 8**
70956-2 ($4.99 US/ $6.99 Can)

☐ **RIBSY**
70955-4 ($4.99 US/ $6.99 Can)

☐ **STRIDER**
71236-9 ($4.99 US/ $6.99 Can)

☐ **HENRY AND THE PAPER ROUTE**
70921-X ($4.99 US/ $6.99 Can)

☐ **RAMONA AND HER MOTHER**
70952-X ($4.99 US/ $6.99 Can)

☐ **OTIS SPOFFORD**
70919-8 ($4.99 US/ $7.50 Can)

☑ **THE MOUSE AND THE MOTORCYCLE**
70924-4 ($4.99 US/ $6.99 Can)

☐ **SOCKS**
70926-0 ($4.99 US/ $6.99 Can)

☐ **EMILY'S RUNAWAY IMAGINATION**
70923-6 ($4.99 US/ $6.99 Can)

☐ **MUGGIE MAGGIE**
71087-0 ($4.99 US/ $7.50 Can)

☑ **RAMONA THE PEST**
70954-6 ($4.99 US/ $6.99 Can)

☐ **RALPH S. MOUSE**
70957-0 ($4.99 US/ $6.99 Can)

☐ **DEAR MR. HENSHAW**
70958-9 ($4.99 US/ $6.99 Can)

☑ **RAMONA THE BRAVE**
70959-7 ($4.99 US/ $6.99 Can)

☐ **RAMONA FOREVER**
70960-0 ($4.99 US/ $6.99 Can)

☐ **FIFTEEN**
72804-4/$4.99 US/ $6.99 Can

☐ **JEAN AND JOHNNY**
72805-2/$4.99 US/ $6.99 Can

☐ **THE LUCKIEST GIRL**
72806-0/$4.99 US/ $6.99 Can

☐ **SISTER OF THE BRIDE**
72807-9/$4.99 US/ $6.99 Can

Buy these books at your local bookstore or use this coupon for ordering:

Mail to: Avon Books/HarperCollins Publishers, P.O. Box 588, Scranton, PA 18512   H
Please send me the book(s) I have checked above.
❑ My check or money order—no cash or CODs please—for $_____is enclosed (please add $1.50 per order to cover postage and handling—Canadian residents add 7% GST). U.S. and Canada residents make checks payable to HarperCollins Publishers Inc.
❑ Charge my VISA/MC Acct#_____Exp Date_____
Minimum credit card order is two books or $7.50 (please add postage and handling charge of $1.50 per order—Canadian residents add 7% GST). For faster service, call 1-800-331-3761. Prices and numbers are subject to change without notice. Please allow six to eight weeks for delivery.

Name_____
Address_____
City_____State/Zip_____
Telephone No._____   BEV 0899